*Dream big, start small.*

Make waves *
Daniella Appolonia

For information about special discounts for bulk purchases,
events, or live readings, please contact
daniellaappolonia@gmail.com.

For more information, visit www.iamdaphnebook.com
and follow the Instagram @iamdaphne_book.

The text for this book was set in Archerus Grotesque.

Some characters and events in this book are fictitious. Any similarity to
real persons, living or dead, is coincidental and not intended by the author.

ISBN 978-1-79-098199-1 (Paperback Edition)
ISBN 978-0-578-50312-7 (Hardcover Edition)

Editing by Sonia Black & Annabel Lee
All book illustrations and cover design by Phoebe Feng

First printing May 2020

eBook edition also available

# I AM DAPHNE

STORY & WORDS
## DANIELLA APPOLONIA

ILLUSTRATIONS
## PHOEBE FENG

LITTLE MOON PRESS

See all the children
so big and so tall?
Daphne isn't like them.
Daphne is very small.

The kids in the playground:
they lunge and they leap.
Like frogs in the jungle,
up branches they creep.

But Daphne just swings.
Whee! Watch her soar!
She wants to fly free,
being small is a bore.

Tiny legs can get tired
running fast for tag.
Playing hide and seek,
no one finds her – what a drag!

She can't climb up trees,
or reach books on a shelf.

STAR POWER

THE LAST FRONTIER

CONSTELLATIONS

Even on her tippy toes,
she's tiny as an elf.

Daphne dreams of growing.
She stretches and strains.

If she stretches far enough,
her height might change!

To cheer up little Daphne
Mom takes her to the zoo.
Daphne starts to feel different.
She's happy, not blue.

They wave to animals,
see creatures big and small.
Daphne runs to the giraffes,
wishing she could be tall.

Dad thinks she's perfect,
and wishes Daphne knew.
But he simply tells her,
"Small things matter too!"

Daphne thinks she's grown,
checking lines on the wall.
Her brother keeps sprouting,
but Daphne is still small.

"I'll drink my milk,"
said Daphne.

"And eat my Brussels sprouts!"

"So I'll grow big and tall...
I've got it all figured out."

The seasons change,
and the years fly by.
Daphne doesn't grow an inch,
and she doesn't know why.

Mom thinks it's time
for a true tale of outer space.
"There's a tiny moon," she said,
"the eye can't even trace."

"But astronauts see it
make huge waves in each ring
around the planet Saturn,
a much bigger thing."

"What's the moon called?"
Daphne asked, perking up.
"Daphnis," Mom answered.
"That's what you're named after, pup."

"You were tiny from the start," she said,
"and still tiny now...
but you'll make waves, dear,
just like Daphnis, somehow."

"Imagine that!" Mom said with a wink.
"A little moon doing something so GREAT!"
Daphne smiled. She finally knew
no one waits to make waves: you just do.

That moon wasn't scared,
of being so small.
Maybe small wasn't
so bad after all.

From that day on,
Daphne knew in her heart,
all the things she wanted,
she could do from the start.

If ever she doubted
each hope and each dream,
she thought about Daphnis,
and began to beam.

"I am Daphne!" she cried
from the top of a tree.
"I am Daphne!" she shouted,
her arms spread with glee.

"I am Daphne!" she yelled,
as she tagged the kids fast.
"I am Daphne!" she shouted,
feeling free at last.

If you hear, "You're so little!"
and it makes you feel bad,
just shoot for the moon, kid,
and show them you're rad.

It's delightful to be different
on Earth's big spinning ball.
You can do GREAT things: you can!
That's what matters, after all.

Thank you to my mother, my father, and my sister and brother — none of this would be possible without your encouragement and unyielding belief in me. Thank you to the Percocos for always keeping my heart full. To my Nonno, and my Nonna in heaven: thank you for teaching me sensitivity, strength, and passion.

Thank you to my Aunt Ann for always supporting my latest writing adventures. Cheryl Racanelli: thank you for your wisdom and encouragement, writer to writer.

Sonia Black: no thanks is big enough for the countless hours you spent validating my words and helping to craft this story. Your grace and generosity are unsurpassed.

Annabel Lee: I am so incredibly lucky I get to learn from you. I appreciate your friendship, wisdom, and guidance more than you know.

Phoebe Feng: thank you, thank you, thank you for being my partner in crime, for believing in this, and for being a wonderful person to make cool stuff with.

To my greatest teachers throughout my life: Reynold Forman and Betty Lou Blumberg. Thank you for pushing me to be better and helping my love of the written word flourish.

And, last but not least, thank you to Daphnis: a beautiful little moon in space who found me at just the right time, when I needed her most.

~D.A.

Thank you to my mom for encouraging my love of the arts, and to my dad for quietly supporting me and pushing me to aim for the best.

~P.F.

## DANIELLA APPOLONIA

is a writer based in New Jersey.
Her nose is always in a book and she's
beyond excited to have created a story
of her own. *I Am Daphne* is her first book.
Visit daniellaappolonia.com to see more
of her writing.

## PHOEBE FENG

is a New York-based designer, illustrator,
and foodie. She drew on desks in school
with pencils instead of permanent markers
to be 'responsible.' She still got sent to
the Principal's office, but it was clearly
all worth it. Visit phoebefeng.com to see
more of her design work.

Made in the USA
Middletown, DE
22 July 2022